THE JUNIOR NOVELIZATION

Library of Congress Control Number: 2009930598
ISBN: 978-0-7364-2711-1
www.randomhouse.com/kids
Printed in the United States of America
10 9 8 7 6 5 4 3 2

DISNEY · PIXAR

TOY STORY 3

THE JUNIOR NOVELIZATION

Adapted by Jasmine Jones

Random House  New York

CHAPTER ONE

"Okay, places, everyone. Get in position," Woody the cowboy said in a hushed voice.

The toys shifted around nervously. It was dark inside Andy's toy box, but a sliver of light crept in through the slightly open lid.

Woody glanced at his best friend, Buzz Lightyear, a space ranger toy. Woody and Buzz had come up with the plan—and now they just hoped it would work. This was the toys' last chance, and they all knew it.

"There they are!" Rex clapped his tiny plastic tyrannosaurus hands as Sarge and two small Green Army Men trooped into Andy's room. They were dragging a gym sock behind them.

"Mission accomplished!" Sarge called as he and his soldiers hoisted the sock up to Buzz. The space ranger pulled it over the edge of the toy box.

Buzz turned the sock upside down. A cell phone slid out. The toys gathered around it.

"Everyone ready?" Woody asked.

"We're ready, Woody!" Jessie answered. "Let's do it!" The red-haired cowgirl flashed a smile.

"Okay." Woody nodded. "Make the call."

Buzz flipped open the cover of his wrist communicator. The number of Andy's cell phone was written there. Jessie pulled out the cordless phone they'd swiped from the kitchen earlier that day. She punched in Andy's number.

Woody tossed the cell phone to Rex as it started to ring. The toys held their breath. They heard footsteps on the stairs! Coming up the hall! Now the footsteps were right outside the door!

"Target is on approach," Buzz murmured.

"Just like we rehearsed it, guys," Woody said, lowering the toy box lid.

The door creaked as Andy entered the room. The toys could hear him shuffling around, looking for his phone. Suddenly, light flooded the toys' eyes as the lid of the toy box opened. Andy peered down. The toys lay frozen, smiling up at him with eager faces. All they wanted was for Andy to play with them.

The trouble was, Andy wasn't a kid anymore. He was a six-foot-tall teenager with shaggy hair. But the toys still hoped for one more playtime. It had been so long!

Andy rummaged through the box, searching for his phone. At last he found it, stuck between Rex's arms. Andy picked up the dinosaur and pulled the phone free.

"Hello?" Andy said into the phone. "Hello? Anyone there?"

No answer. With a shrug, Andy hung up. "Molly, stay out of my room!" he shouted at his little sister.

"I wasn't in your room!" she shouted back from down the hall.

Andy rolled his eyes, then looked down at Rex, who was still in his hand.

The toys watched eagerly. Was this it? Was their plan going to work?

Andy dropped Rex back into the toy box. He shut the lid and left the room.

The toys were heartbroken. "Well, that went well," Mr. Potato Head said sarcastically as they all spilled out into Andy's room.

"He actually held me!" Rex shouted, hopping up and down with joy.

"Aw, who are we kidding?" Mr. Potato Head moaned.

"We aren't ever getting played with," Slinky said, shaking his head sadly.

Deep down, Woody knew they were right. He glanced at Buzz, who nodded.

"I'm calling it, guys," Woody told his friends. "Andy's going to college any day now. That was our last shot."

"We're going into Attic Mode, folks," Buzz explained, stepping up next to Woody.

The toys gasped. Then they all began to argue. No one wanted to go into the attic.

"Hey, hey, now, come on, guys." Woody held up his hands. "We all knew this day was coming. Every toy goes through this. No one wants to see their kid grow up and leave."

"Hey! Sarge!" Buzz called out suddenly. "What are you doing?"

The toys all turned. Sarge and his soldiers were up on the windowsill. "War's over, folks," said Sarge. "Me and the boys are moving on."

"You're going AWOL?" Buzz looked stunned. The army guys were deserting them?

"We've done our duty," Sarge said. "Andy's grown up."

9

"And let's face it," a soldier added. "When the trash bags come out, we Army guys are the first to go."

Sarge gave Woody a salute. "It has been an honor serving with you. Good luck, folks."

The toy soldiers parachuted out the window, and the wind carried them away.

"We're getting thrown away?" Rex cried. He looked terrified.

"No!" Woody insisted. "No one's getting thrown away!"

But the toys weren't listening. "We're being abandoned!" Jessie gasped. Everyone started to panic.

"Whoa! Hold on! Quiet!" Woody waved his arms, silencing them. "No one's getting thrown out, okay? We're all still here, aren't we? I mean, we've lost friends along the way—but through every yard sale, every spring cleaning, Andy held on to us. He must care about us or we wouldn't *be* here. You wait—Andy's going to tuck us in the attic. It'll be safe and warm . . ."

"And we'll all be together," Buzz added.

"Exactly," Woody replied.

The toys murmured, nodding. It didn't sound so bad when Woody put it that way.

"Come on, guys," Buzz said. "Let's get our parts together, get ready, and go out on a high note."

Mrs. Potato Head sighed. "I'd better find my other eye."

"Where'd you leave it this time?" her husband asked.

Mrs. Potato Head clamped a hand over her remaining eye and squinted. Now she could see through the lost eye. "Someplace dusty," she replied.

"Don't worry," Woody called as the toys tramped away. He smiled confidently. "Andy's gonna take care of us. I guarantee it."

Woody climbed onto Andy's desk. On the corkboard, behind Andy's high school graduation photo, was a picture of Andy as a child. He was holding Woody and Buzz. They were surrounded by the other toys.

Woody stared longingly at the photo. In those days, Andy had played with them for hours at a time. Woody wished things could go back to the way they had been then.

"You guarantee it, huh?" Buzz asked, coming up next to him.

Woody sighed. "I don't know, Buzz. What else could I say?"

Buzz put a reassuring hand on Woody's shoulder. "Whatever happens, at least we'll be together."

Woody gazed at the photo of Andy and nodded. "For infinity . . . and beyond."

CHAPTER TWO

The toys heard voices in the hallway. Gasping, they scrambled back to the toy box. They dived inside just as the door swung open. Andy walked into the room with his sister, Molly.

"Can I have your computer?" she begged. "Your video games?"

"Forget it, Molly," Andy said as he sat down at his laptop computer and started typing. Just then, their mom walked into the room. She was carrying cardboard boxes and trash bags.

"Andy, let's get to work here," she said brightly, placing the boxes on Andy's bed. "Anything you're not taking to college either goes in the attic, or it's trash."

Andy didn't look up from the computer. "Mom, I'm not leaving until Friday."

Andy's mom picked up his skateboard. "Look, it's simple. Skateboard?" She dumped it a box. "College. Little League trophy? Probably attic. Apple core? Trash." She picked up an ancient apple core from Andy's dresser and tossed it into one of the trash bags. "You can do the rest."

Molly peered into the toy box. "Why do you still have these toys?" she sneered.

"You're not off the hook, either, Molly!" their mom said as Molly flounced out the door. Mrs. Davis wrote SUNNYSIDE on an empty box, then dropped it in Molly's room. "You have more toys than you know what to do with. Some of them could make other kids really happy. The daycare is always asking for donations."

Molly pouted. "But, Mom . . ."

Mrs. Davis held firm. "No buts. You choose the toys you want to donate. I'll drop them off at Sunnyside."

She turned and walked down the hall.

With a sigh, Molly looked around her room. She chose an old rainbow-colored xylophone and tossed it into the box marked for donation.

From across the hall, Andy's toys watched as Molly picked up her Barbie doll and studied her sweet, smiling face. With a shrug, Molly tossed the Barbie into the box, too.

"Poor Barbie!" Jessie whispered.

"I get the Corvette," said Hamm.

Andy's mom walked back into his room. He was still typing away on the computer. "Andy, come on—what are you going to do with these toys?" She opened the toy box. "Should we donate them to Sunnyside?"

"No," Andy replied.

"Maybe sell them online?" Mrs. Davis suggested.

Andy rolled his eyes. "Mom, no one's gonna want those old toys," he said. "They're junk!"

Junk? The word hit Andy's toys like a slap. They'd always thought of themselves as Andy's *friends*.

"Fine, you have till Friday," Andy's mom told him. "Anything that's not packed for college or in the attic is getting thrown out."

Once his mother had left the room, Andy closed his laptop with a sigh. He walked over to the toy box and looked down at all his old toys.

Andy grabbed a trash bag and snapped it open. He picked up Rex and stuffed him into the bag. In went the Potato Heads. Jessie. Bullseye. Slinky. The Aliens. Andy uncorked Hamm and emptied the change onto his desk before shoving the piggy bank in with the rest.

Then Andy came to Buzz and Woody. He paused for a moment, looking from one to the other. Finally, he dropped Woody into the box marked COLLEGE. He dropped Buzz into the garbage bag and headed for the door.

Buzz landed on top of the pile of toys. He couldn't

believe it! Andy had just thrown him away!

"What's happening?" Rex cried.

"We're getting thrown out! That's what!" Mr. Potato Head snapped.

Woody jumped out of the COLLEGE box and raced after Andy. He couldn't let his friends get thrown away!

Andy walked into the hall and stopped. Woody hid behind the door frame and watched as Andy reached up and pulled down a trapdoor that released a ladder in the hall's ceiling. Woody sighed with relief. Andy was taking his friends to the attic after all!

Just then, Molly came out of her room, carrying the heavy box of toys she was donating.

"You need a hand?" Andy asked his sister. Setting down the garbage bag, he took the box from Molly and helped her carry it down the stairs.

Inside the garbage bag, the toys were all talking at once. "I can't breathe!" Jessie gasped.

"Quiet!" Buzz commanded. "What's that sound?"

They heard a faint creak. The spring-loaded ladder to the attic was folding back up into the ceiling. It knocked over the bag of toys.

Woody gasped. He hurried into the hall to help his friends. But at that moment, Andy's mom came around the corner. She was carrying a full garbage bag in each hand.

Woody ducked back into Andy's room.

Mrs. Davis tripped over the garbage bag full of toys lying in the hallway. She looked down. "Andy?" she called, annoyed. When there was no answer, she scooped up the bag and carried it downstairs with the rest of the garbage.

"That's not trash!" Woody cried. He ran to the window and saw Andy's mom drop the bag at the curb, right next to the trash cans.

At that moment, a garbage truck rumbled up the street. *I have to help them!* Woody thought desperately. He grabbed a pair of scissors from the desk and slipped them into his holster. Then he ran to the windowsill and jumped toward the drainpipe. He hit the gutter instead and tumbled head over heels into the bushes.

Inside the bag, the toys were terrified.

"We're on the curb!" Jessie shouted.

"There's gotta be a way out!" Buzz insisted. They pulled at the plastic with all their might, but the bag was too strong. They couldn't tear it open.

"Oh, Andy doesn't want us!" Mr. Potato Head groaned. "What's the point?"

"Point . . . ," Buzz repeated, thinking hard. "Point— POINT!" He looked down at Rex's pointy tail. He had an idea!

"I can hear the garbage truck!" Rex cried, his voice quivering with fear. The rest of the toys helped Buzz shove Rex backward against the plastic bag.

Meanwhile, Woody climbed out of the bushes and raced across the yard. He dived behind the mailbox, watching as the garbageman picked up a trash can and emptied it into the truck.

When the man wasn't looking, Woody ducked out from behind the post and plunged his scissors into a garbage bag. Kitchen trash spilled out.

Woody darted back to his hiding place as the garbageman picked up the rest of the bags and tossed them into the truck. The truck started down the street. Woody chased after it.

At the next house, the truck stopped. The garbageman flipped a lever. *Crunch!*

"Buzz!" Woody cried in horror. "Jessie!"

Just then, he heard a sound behind him. Woody turned. A blue recycling bin scurried up Andy's driveway on several tiny plastic feet.

Woody sighed in relief. His friends had escaped! He hurried after them.

Inside the garage, the toys threw off the recycling bin. "Junk!" Mr. Potato Head snapped. "He called us junk!"

"Sarge was right," said Hamm, groaning.

"Yeah!" said Mr. Potato Head. "And Woody was wrong!"

Suddenly, Jessie let out a shout. "Yee-haw! Fellas, I know what to do!" She pointed to the back of the car. The hatchback was open. Inside was a box of Molly's toys, labeled SUNNYSIDE. Andy's toys didn't have to be thrown away—they could be donated!

"Jessie, wait! What about Woody?" Buzz asked as the other toys began to clamber into the box.

"He's fine, Buzz! Andy's taking him to college!" Jessie said, giving one of the Aliens a boost.

Buzz nodded. "You're right. Come on!"

Just then, Woody ran into the garage. "Buzz? What's going on? Don't you know this box is being donated?"

"It's under control, Woody. We have a plan!" Buzz replied, helping Jessie with another Alien.

"We're going to daycare!" Rex cried happily.

"Daycare?" Woody gaped at his friends. "Have you all lost your marbles?"

"Didn't you see?" Mrs. Potato Head wailed. "Andy threw us away!"

"No!" Woody insisted. "That was a mistake! Andy's mom thought you were trash!"

"After he put us in the trash bag," Hamm pointed out.

"And called us junk!" Mrs. Potato Head added.

"I know it looks bad," Woody admitted. "But, guys, you've got to believe me!"

"Andy's moving on, Woody!" Jessie said. "It's time we did the same." She ducked into the box. The toys pulled the flaps shut over their heads.

Woody lost his temper. "Okay, out of the box!" he shouted, climbing into the car.

"Woody—wait!" Buzz said. "We need to figure out what's best for everyone—"

Slam! Suddenly, the hatchback closed. Andy's mom got

into the driver's seat and started the car engine.

"Oh, great!" Woody fumed as the car pulled out of the driveway. "It's gonna take us forever to get back here!"

Woody and Buzz climbed into the box, where the other toys were comforting Molly's Barbie doll. "Okay, everyone, listen up," Woody said. "We'll hide under the seats until we get back home, then—"

"Get it through your vinyl noggin, Woody," Mr. Potato Head growled. "Andy doesn't want us anymore!"

"He was *putting* you in the *attic*!" Woody shouted.

"He *left* us on the *curb*!" Jessie yelled back.

"All right, calm down!" Buzz said, stepping between them. "Both of you!"

"Fine!" Woody threw his hands in the air. "Just wait till you see what daycare is like!"

"Why?" Rex asked. "What's it like?"

"Daycare is a sad, lonely place for washed-up old toys who have no owners," Woody told him.

Barbie burst into tears.

Hamm shook his head at Woody. "Quite the charmer, aren't ya?"

"Oh, you'll see!" Woody warned him.

There were two holes cut into the sides of the box to use as handholds. The toys crowded around one of them, peering out. After a short drive, the car turned into the daycare center's parking lot. No one knew what would come next.

CHAPTER THREE

"**C**an anyone see anything?" Rex asked as the car came to a stop in front of Sunnyside Daycare. The toys looked through the box's handholds.

"There's a playground!" Jessie said, pointing to a whitewashed wall. They could hear children on the other side yelling and laughing.

Hamm turned to Woody. "So much for 'sad and lonely.'"

"Okay, calm down, guys," Woody said. He didn't want the toys to get too excited about Sunnyside. After all, they belonged with Andy.

"Woody, it's nice!" Rex squealed. "See, the door has a rainbow on it!"

Andy's mom took the box and carried it into

the building. A receptionist was sitting at the front desk. A young girl sat on the desk beside her, playing with a toy monkey.

"I just wanted to drop these old toys off," Andy's mom said. She smiled at the little girl and chatted with the receptionist. Andy and Molly had gone to the daycare center when they were little children, so the receptionist knew Mrs. Davis.

After Andy's mom left, the receptionist took the box into one of the classrooms and set it on a counter. As soon as she was gone, the toys scrambled to look at their new home through the box's handholds.

It was a beautiful room painted in cheerful colors. Bright paper butterflies hung from the ceiling. And everywhere the toys looked, there were children playing. To Andy's toys, it looked like heaven.

"Okay, everyone," the teacher called as a bell rang. "Recess!" She opened a door to the playground.

With a cheer, the kids put down their toys and raced outside into the sunshine. The teacher turned off the lights and closed the door behind her.

Andy's toys elbowed one another. Everyone was trying to get a better view.

"Whoa!" Slinky cried as the box tipped forward. It fell off the counter, and Andy's toys spilled out.

The toys that already lived in the classroom turned. For a moment, they gaped at Andy's toys in surprise.

"New toys!" one of the Sunnyside toys cried.

Suddenly, Woody and his friends were surrounded by cheerful toys. Everyone was shaking hands and talking at once.

"Well, howdy!" Jessie said to a jack-in-the-box. "Glad to meetcha!" A muscle-bound action figure with a fly head made Mrs. Potato Head giggle. A bunch of tiny dinosaurs surrounded Rex, looking up at him in awe.

A crane toy circled the Aliens. "The Claw!" they cried.

The crane reminded the Aliens of the claw arcade game at Pizza Planet, where Andy had won them.

A large toy truck zoomed up. It screeched to a stop and spun around. A pink strawberry-scented teddy bear was sitting in the back.

"Well, hello there!" the bear said with an easy smile. "Welcome to Sunnyside, folks! I'm Lots-o'-Huggin' Bear! But please, call me Lotso!"

Buzz stepped forward and held out his hand. "Buzz Lightyear. We come in pea—"

Lotso grabbed Buzz up in a huge bear hug. "First thing you've got to know about me is I'm a hugger!"

Lotso smiled at the rest of Andy's toys. "Look at y'all! You've been through a lot today, haven't you?"

Mrs. Potato Head got a tear in her eye. "Oh, it's been horrible."

"Well, you're safe now," Lotso told her. "We're all cast-offs here. We've been dumped, donated, yard-saled, secondhanded, and just plain thrown out. But just you wait. You'll find being donated was the best thing that ever happened to ya!"

"Mr. Lotso," Rex piped up, "do toys here get played with every day?"

"All day long," Lotso assured him. "Five days a week."

"But what happens when the kids grow up?" asked Jessie.

"Well now, I'll tell you." Lotso led the toys over to a wall covered in classroom photos—year after year of daycare kids. "When the kids get old, new ones come in."

The toys couldn't have hoped for more. "It's a miracle!" Mrs. Potato Head cried.

Her husband nudged Woody. "And you wanted us to stay at Andy's!"

"Because we're Andy's toys!" Woody exclaimed.

Lotso put an arm around Woody's shoulder. "So you got donated by this 'Andy,' huh? Well, it's his loss, Sheriff! He can't hurt you no more," the bear said.

Woody shook his head. Lotso had it all wrong. Andy would never hurt them!

But Lotso wasn't listening. "Now, let's get you all settled in," he said, turning to the others. "Ken?" he called. "Where is that boy? Ken? New toys!"

A Ken doll appeared in the upstairs window of a dollhouse. "Far out!" he exclaimed. Ken took the dollhouse elevator to the first floor and walked out, flashing a brilliant smile.

"Folks, if you wanna step right this wa—" Turning, Ken came face to face with Barbie. His eyes widened. "Hi! I'm Ken."

"Barbie," she said breathlessly. They stared at each other. It was love at first sight!

Lotso finally pulled Ken and Barbie apart. "Come on, Ken. Recess don't last forever!"

"Right on, Lotso!" Ken said, shaking off the spell that

Barbie had cast over him. "This way, everybody!"

"You got a lot to look forward to, folks," Lotso said, beaming. "The little ones love new toys!"

"What a nice bear!" Buzz remarked as they followed Ken and Lotso.

"And he smells like strawberries!" Rex added.

Woody sighed, exasperated.

"Here at Sunnyside, we've got just about anything a toy could ask for," Ken announced as he led them on a tour of the room.

Lotso pointed out shelves of containers filled with supplies. "Spare parts, superglue, and enough fresh batteries to choke a hippo."

Ken opened a closet door, revealing a workshop. Toys were busy stitching rips, combing tangled hair, adding stuffing, and polishing plastic.

"Our repair shop will keep you stuffed, puffed, and lightly buffed!" Ken explained to Andy's toys.

They arrived back at Ken's dollhouse. "And this, well, this is where I live. It has a disco, a dune buggy, and a whole room just for trying on clothes."

Barbie gasped. "You have everything!"

"Except someone to share it with," Ken said. He gave Barbie a shy look, then walked ahead.

Barbie sighed dreamily.

"You need anything at all," Lotso said as they reached the end of the room, "you just come talk to me. Here we are!" Lotso knocked on the door of a bathroom. A gigantic baby doll opened the door. He was covered with ballpoint pen tattoos. Andy's toys stared, not sure what to make of the tough-looking doll.

"Well, thank you, Big Baby," Lotso said to the doll. "Why don't you come meet our new friends?"

Big Baby cooed at Andy's toys.

"Poor Baby," Lotso said in a low voice. "We were thrown out together. Abandoned by the same owner!"

The pink bear led Andy's toys through the bathroom and into another classroom. "And here's where you folks will be staying—the Caterpillar Room!"

Andy's toys gazed around them. The room was decorated with finger paintings. There were building blocks, art supplies, tiny tables and chairs, and toys everywhere.

"Look at this place!" Jessie said. Buzz let out a low whistle.

Ding! Ding! Woody looked down. A toy telephone bumped against his boot. "Hey, little fella," Woody said. The toy rolled over his boot again. *Ding! Ding!*

"In a few minutes that bell's gonna ring, and you'll get the playtime that you've been dreaming of," Lotso told Andy's toys.

Rex could hardly contain his excitement. "Real play! I can't wait!"

"Now, if you'll excuse us, we best be heading back," Lotso said. He climbed into the truck that was waiting for him. "Welcome to Sunnyside, folks!"

Ken grabbed Barbie's hands. "Barbie, come with me! I know we've just met, but when I look at you I feel like we were . . ."

". . . made for each other!" Barbie and Ken cried in unison. They both gasped. Barbie said goodbye to her friends. Then they hurried over to the truck and climbed in back with Lotso. The truck roared off. Big Baby closed the door behind them.

The toys could hear children laughing and playing outside. "Why can't time go faster?" Rex cried.

Woody stepped forward. "Look, everyone, it's nice here, I admit," he said. "But we need to go home now."

His friends glanced at one another. Was he crazy? "We can have a new life here, Woody," Jessie told him. "A chance to make kids happy again."

"Why don't you stay?" Slinky urged.

"I can't!" Woody cried. "I have a kid. *You* have a kid—

Andy! If he wants us at college, or in the attic, then that's where we should be! Now, I'm going home. Anyone who wants to join me is welcome! Come on, Buzz!"

He started to walk off, but Buzz didn't follow.

Woody turned. "Buzz?"

The space ranger looked at him sadly. "Our mission with Andy is complete, Woody. . . ."

"How can you say that?" Woody cried.

"And what's important now is that we stay together," Buzz finished.

"We wouldn't even *be* together if it weren't for Andy!" Woody pointed to Buzz's foot. "Look under your boot, Buzz! You too, Jessie! Whose name is written there, huh?"

The toys stared at the ground. Finally Rex said what they were all thinking. "Maybe Andy doesn't care about us anymore."

Woody was shocked. "Of course he does!"

"Woody, *wake up!*" Jessie raised her voice in frustration.

"It's over! Andy is *all grown up!*"

"I can't believe how selfish you all are," Woody snapped, glaring at his friends. "So this is it? After all we've been through?"

Buzz stepped forward and held out his hand. But Woody didn't shake it. Instead, he straightened his hat and headed for the door. Bullseye trailed after him.

"Bullseye, no," Woody told the trusty horse. "You need to stay."

He turned toward the door again, and again Bullseye followed him.

"Bullseye, no, I said *stay!*" Woody's voice sounded harsher than he meant it to. "Look," he added gently. "I don't want you left alone in the attic, okay? Now, stay." He patted the horse.

Keys jingled in the lock. Someone was at the door.

"I gotta go," Woody told his friends.

The receptionist opened the door and walked into the

classroom. Woody slipped through the open door and into the hallway. A janitor almost saw him, but Woody grabbed on to the underside of a rolling trash cart. The janitor wheeled the cart through the lobby, toward the exit. But at the last moment, the janitor veered off toward the bathroom.

"No!" Woody cried, frustrated.

When the janitor started cleaning the sinks, Woody sneaked into a toilet stall. There was an open window over the tank.

Carefully, Woody climbed onto the toilet tank. He hauled himself outside through the window and climbed up a drainpipe. From there he scrambled onto the roof.

But when he looked down, he saw that the daycare center's high wall was too far away for him to jump over. Woody frowned. How would he get out?

Suddenly, a gust of wind blew his hat off. Woody chased it as it skidded across the roof. The hat landed underneath a kite that was tangled in a gutter. That gave Woody an idea.

The cowboy settled his hat back on his head. Then he grabbed the kite and held it overhead like a hang glider. He ran across the roof and leaped. Woody soared over the playground and landed outside the wall. The cowboy laughed in triumph. He'd made it!

But before he could let go of the kite, another gust of wind yanked him back into the air. He rose higher and higher. The kite dipped and swirled. Woody clung to the crossbar, hanging on for dear life.

Snap!

The crossbar broke. Woody yelped as he plunged toward the ground. He crashed into a tree. His hat flew off as he tumbled through the branches. He came to a stop just inches from the ground.

Slowly, Woody opened one eye, then the other. He was safe! But he was stuck. His pull string had caught on a branch. That was what had broken his fall.

"Reach for the sky!" Woody's voice box said as he

swung around, struggling to free the string.

At that moment, the receptionist's daughter, Bonnie, looked up from her game of hopscotch. She saw Woody dangling right in front of her. She glanced around, clearly wondering if he belonged to anyone. But no one else was nearby. Bonnie tugged Woody from the tree. "You're my favorite deputy!" his voice box said as his string snapped back into place.

"Bonnie!" her mother called from the car. She honked the horn.

"I'm coming!" Bonnie shoved Woody into her backpack and ran to meet her mother.

"Oh, great!" Woody groaned inside the bag as the car pulled away. Who knew where he was headed now?

Andy was going to college soon—and if Woody couldn't find a way home, Andy would leave without him!

CHAPTER FOUR

Back in the Caterpillar Room, Bullseye whinnied sadly. Jessie patted him. She knew he missed Woody. "Oh, it's going to be okay, Bullseye."

"Woody's going to college with Andy," Buzz added. "It's what he always wanted."

"Oooh!" Hamm said from the windowsill. He was watching the kids on the playground. "They're lining up out there!"

"Places, everyone!" Buzz called.

The bell rang. The toys heard kids yelling and laughing in the hallway. Footsteps pounded toward the door.

"At last!" Rex shouted, spreading his arms wide. "I'm gonna get played with!" He faced the door. "Come to Papa!"

Buzz looked around. He noticed that the other Caterpillar Room toys were edging away from the door. They ducked into cubbies and hid behind the furniture.

Something wasn't right. Buzz was starting to warn his friend, when the doors flew open, swatting Rex across the room. The toys went limp as a group of toddlers thundered in. Eager hands grabbed Andy's toys.

A girl and a boy stretched Slinky much too far. A boy jammed Mrs. Potato Head into a train and smashed it into a wall so all her parts flew off. A little girl used Jessie's hair as a paintbrush. Another little girl covered Hamm in glue, glitter, and dried macaroni.

A girl was using Buzz's head as a hammer until a boy stole the paper crown she was wearing. She screamed and tossed Buzz away. He landed on the windowsill, where he could see across the courtyard into the Butterfly Room.

It was a completely different world. In the Butterfly Room, the children held Lotso and his friends while the teacher read to them. The kids cuddled the toys lovingly.

It really was heaven in there. But here—

A boy's hand reached up and grabbed Buzz, pulling him back into the fray.

"There's a snake in my boot!" Woody's voice box announced. He was in Bonnie's room.

Bonnie pulled his string again. "I'd like to join your posse, boys, but first I'm gonna sing a little song," said Woody's voice box.

Bonnie smiled. "A sheriff!" She set Woody in a chair at a table surrounded by stuffed animals.

"Move over, Mr. Pricklepants!" Bonnie said, pushing aside a hedgehog in lederhosen. "We have a guest!" Bonnie hopped from foot to foot. "You want some coffee?" She set out some cups and pretended to pour from a pitcher. "It's good for you, but don't drink too much or you'll have to—

Be right back!" Bonnie darted out the door.

As soon as she was gone, Woody looked around. The other toys were still frozen in place. "Pssst! Hey! Hello!" Woody whispered to the white unicorn across from him. "Can you tell me where I am?"

The hedgehog shushed Woody.

"The guy's just asking a question," the unicorn said.

"Well, excuse me!" huffed the hedgehog. "I am trying to stay in character!"

"My name's Buttercup," the unicorn told Woody.

The hedgehog shushed him.

"I'm Trixie," put in a plastic triceratops.

Mr. Pricklepants scowled at her. "Shhh!"

Trixie shushed him right back.

Woody waved, trying to get their attention. "Guys, hey! Look, I don't know where I am. . . ."

"We're either in a café in Paris or a coffee shop in New Jersey," Trixie told him.

"We do a lot of improv here," Buttercup explained. "Just stay loose, have fun, and you'll be fine!"

Woody shook his head. These toys didn't understand! But before he could ask again, a toilet flushed. Bonnie ran back into the room.

"Who wants lunch?" She pushed the buttons on a toy microwave, then pulled out a plate. She placed a plastic hamburger in front of Woody. "It has a secret ingredient," she said, lifting the bun to show him. "Jelly beans!" She popped a candy into her mouth and pulled Woody's string again.

"Somebody's poisoned the water hole!" his voice box announced.

Bonnie spat out the jellybean. "Poison? Who would do such a mean thing?" She turned and picked up another doll, then let out an evil-sounding cackle. *"Hee-hee-hee-hee-hee!* The scary witch!" Bonnie flew the witch around the room. "Look out!"

Bonnie ran into her closet. "We need a spaceship to get away from the witch!"

While she was gone, Trixie leaned over to Woody. "You're doing great!"

"Are you classically trained?" Mr. Pricklepants asked.

"Look," Woody said, "I just need to get out of here—"

"There is no way out!" Buttercup cried dramatically.

Woody stared at him in horror.

"Just kidding," the unicorn said. "Door's right over there."

"I found the spaceship!" Bonnie cried. The toys went limp as she darted out of the closet. She was carrying a rocket made from a shoe box.

"Quick, get in!" Bonnie said in Woody's voice. "Fasten your seat belts! Close your tray tables!" She shoved all the toys into the box. Then she put the box on a bedsheet. "Hold on, it might get a little bumpy! Three. Two. One. Blastoff!" Bonnie yanked the sheet, sending the toys flying into the air.

Everyone landed on the bed. "Yee-haw!" Bonnie hugged Woody tight. "You did it, cowboy! You saved us!"

Woody smiled at the other toys. He couldn't remember the last time he'd enjoyed himself so much.

"Oh, I've got a kink in my slink!" Slinky groaned. He looked around at his friends, who were scattered across the floor of the Caterpillar Room.

"My tail!" Rex cried. "Where's my tail?"

The Potato Heads sorted through their parts. The little kids had mixed them all up!

"I don't recall playtime being quite that strenuous," Buzz said, cracking his back.

"Andy never played with us like that!" Rex complained as he pulled his tail out of a pegboard.

The toys looked at one another. What could they do? "We have to make the best of it," Jessie said finally.

"We should be in the Butterfly Room!" Mrs. Potato Head griped. "With the big kids!"

"We'll get this straightened out," Buzz promised. "I'll go talk to Lotso about moving us to the other room."

Buzz strode over to the bathroom door. He climbed a table and leaped to the doorknob. He jumped up and down on it, but it wouldn't budge. "Blast. Try that one!" He pointed to the hallway door.

Jessie leaped and caught the knob. "It's locked!"

"Same here!" Slinky cried from the door to the playground.

Buzz dropped to the floor. "Try the windows."

Hamm examined the lock with a knowing eye. "Eh, negatory. It's a Fenster Schneckler three-eighty—finest childproof lock in the world."

Mrs. Potato Head's eye widened in horror and she cried, "We're trapped!"

"Wait!" Buzz said. "Did anyone notice the transom?"

He pointed at the little window over the door to the hallway. It was open!

Mr. Potato Head groaned. "Oh, great! How do we get up there?"

Buzz led everyone to a push toy, which had a handle and wheels like a lawn mower. "All right, everyone! On three! One. Two . . ."

"Three!" Jessie shouted.

Andy's toys raced at top speed, pushing the toy as fast as it would roll.

"Let go!" Jessie hollered. The toys fell back. Buzz hopped onto the handle as the toy zoomed forward.

The push toy hit a table, launching Buzz into the air. Overhead was a long clothesline that held children's artwork. Buzz grabbed the line, sending paintings flying. He zipped down the line. When he reached the end, he bounced off a broom handle, opened his wings, and soared to the transom.

"He did it!" Rex cried.

"Way to go, Buzz!" Jessie cheered as Buzz unwound a piece of yarn he'd brought with him. He tossed it down to his friends.

They all held tight to one end of the yarn. Tying the other end around his waist, Buzz was just about to use it to climb down into the hall when he heard voices. He paused.

"You think they had a fun playtime?" Chunk, a rock monster toy, said as he swaggered down the hall. He was with Twitch, the action figure with the fly's head.

"Shhh!" Twitch said. "They might hear you."

Buzz frowned. Down the hall, Ken and Barbie were saying goodnight at the door of the Butterfly Room. The two action figures pulled Ken away.

"Come on, Romeo," Twitch said. "We're late."

Ken and the tough toys disappeared into the darkened teachers' lounge.

Quietly, Buzz climbed down to the floor. He untied the

49

yarn from his waist and hurried after them.

Ken, Twitch, and Chunk walked over to a vending machine. Ken opened a flap in the bottom and they went inside.

Buzz followed them. Inside the machine, he saw Twitch, Chunk, Ken, Stretch the rubber octopus toy, and Sparks the robot. They were all clustered around a table, playing games and betting with play money, batteries, and other trinkets. Buzz hid in the shadows, watching.

"Hey, what do you guys think of the new recruits?" Ken asked as the toys placed wagers. "Any keepers?"

"Chuck 'em in the landfill," Stretch scoffed.

"Toddler fodder!" Twitch growled.

"What about that space guy?" Ken asked. "He could be useful."

Buzz started. They were talking about *him*!

"All them toys are disposable," Twitch announced. "We'll be lucky if they last us a week!"

Buzz was shocked. *Disposable? A week?* He had to warn the others! But when he turned around, he ran right into Big Baby.

The giant baby doll picked Buzz up and tossed him into the light. Twitch and Chunk grabbed him.

"Well, well," Ken said. "Looky who we have here."

"Let me go!" Buzz shouted.

"Take him to the library," Ken commanded.

"Nooo!" Buzz hollered as a sock puppet was yanked over his head. But no one could hear him scream.

CHAPTER FIVE

At that moment, Bonnie was sleeping peacefully in her bed. All her toys were tucked in beside her. Woody slipped out of bed and over to her backpack. Bonnie's address was written on the name tag.

"Twelve Twenty-five Sycamore!" Woody murmured.

"Pssst!" Mr. Pricklepants called from the bed. "Woody! What're you doing?"

"I gotta get out of here!" Woody replied.

The toys looked astonished. "Didn't you have fun today?" Buttercup asked.

"Oh, of course I did! More than I've had in years. But, you see, I belong to someone else." Woody showed them Andy's name written on the bottom of his boot. "He's my

Bonnie, and he's leaving soon. I've got to get home!"

"Where's home?" asked one of the peas in a plush pea pod toy.

"Elm Street. Two Thirty-four Elm." Woody thought for a moment. "You guys have a map?"

Meanwhile, back at Sunnyside, Buzz was tied to a chair. Ken, Big Baby, and the other toys had taken him to a utility closet.

"I demand to talk to Lotso," Buzz boomed.

"Zip it, Buck Rogers!" Ken snapped. "You don't talk to Lotso till we say you can."

Just then, the door flew open. Lotso was standing there, clearly shocked. "Ken? Why is this toy tied up?"

"Uh . . . he—he—" Ken stammered. "He got out, Lotso!"

"Got out? Oh, no! This isn't how we treat our guests!" Lotso closed the door. He walked over to Buzz and started untying him. "There you go. I'm so sorry."

Buzz glared at Ken, then turned to the pink bear. "Lotso, there's been a mistake. The children in the Caterpillar Room are not age-appropriate for me and my friends," Buzz explained. "We respectfully request a transfer to the Butterfly Room."

Lotso beamed. "Well, request granted!"

"But, Lotso—" Ken protested.

"Hush now, Kenneth!" Lotso said. "This toy's shown initiative! Leadership! Why, I'd say we found ourselves a keeper! Hear that, everyone? We got a keeper!"

"Excellent!" Buzz grinned. "I'll go get my friends."

He started off, but Lotso stood in his way. "Whoa, whoa . . . Hold on there, boss! Those Caterpillar kids need *someone* to play with!"

Buzz's face fell. "But my friends don't belong there!"

"Oh, none of us do!" Lotso nodded. "I agree! Which is why—for the good of our community—we ask the newer toys, the stronger ones, to take on the hardships the rest of us can't bear anymore." .

Buzz frowned, wondering what to do. "Well, I guess that makes sense. But I can't accept." If the others were stuck in the Caterpillar Room, he would not abandon them. "We're a family—we stay together."

Lotso's smile faded. "Family man, eh? I understand." His eyes narrowed. He nodded sharply to Big Baby. "Put him back in the time-out chair."

The giant baby doll grabbed Buzz and pinned the space ranger to the chair.

"What?" Buzz struggled, but Big Baby was too strong. "Unhand me!"

Lotso turned to Ken. "Bring in the Bookworm."

Ken let out a whistle. Everyone looked up, toward a rustling sound. The top shelves in the closet were cluttered with toy manuals. Suddenly, an ancient toy bookworm appeared between the booklets. The Bookworm tossed a

Buzz Lightyear instruction manual to Lotso.

Lotso flipped it open. "Here we go! 'Remove screws to access battery compartment,'" he read.

Big Baby and Twitch pushed Buzz to the floor. "What are you doing?" Buzz cried as Sparks the robot opened up his battery compartment.

"'To return your Buzz Lightyear action figure to its original factory settings,'" Lotso read, "'slide the switch from Play to Demo.'"

"Stop!" Buzz shouted. He struggled, but Big Baby held him tight. Twitch reached for the switch on Buzz's back.

"Noooo!" Buzz's shout echoed down the hall.

"What was that?" Jessie asked. She and her friends in the Caterpillar Room looked at one another. They'd all heard the noise.

"Sounds like it came from the hall!" Hamm said.

Mrs. Potato Head plucked out her eye. "I'll see what it was!" Holding her eye in one hand, she put it under the door and moved it back and forth. The other toys gathered around her.

Mrs. Potato Head gasped. "I see Andy!"

"What?" Jessie cried.

Mr. Potato Head looked doubtful. "That's impossible!"

"No, no," his wife insisted, "I really see him! In his room!" She thought for a moment, wondering how it was possible. "My other eye!" she said. "The one I left behind."

She squinted, concentrating on the scene in Andy's room. "Andy's out in the hall," she told the toys. "He's looking in the attic. Wait, why is he so upset?"

Mrs. Potato Head saw Andy talking to his mother. He pointed to the spot right below the attic ladder. It was the place where he'd left the toys. He picked up a trash bag and showed it to his mother.

"Oh, no!" Mrs. Potato Head cried. "Oh, this is terrible!"

She put her eye back in and turned to the other toys. "Andy's looking for us! I think he *did* mean to put us in the attic!" she said.

"Woody was telling the truth!" Slinky said.

"Guys, we gotta go home!" Jessie declared.

But just then, the bathroom door creaked open. Lotso and his gang sauntered in.

"How are y'all doing this fine evening?" Lotso asked.

"Lotso!" Jessie rushed over to him. "Thank heavens! Have you seen Buzz?" The other toys joined her, crowding around.

"There's been a mistake!" Mrs. Potato Head explained. "We have to go!"

"Go?" Lotso looked surprised. "Why, you just got here! In the nick of time, too! We were runnin' low on volunteers for the little ones!" He smiled, but it wasn't a nice smile at all. "They just love new toys."

"Love?" Mr. Potato Head said with a scowl. "We've

been chewed! Kicked! Drooled on!"

"Just look at my pocketbook!" Mrs. Potato Head held it out. The purse was covered in tooth marks.

Lotso put his face close to hers. "Here's the thing, Sweet Potato—you ain't leavin' Sunnyside."

"Sweet Potato?" Mrs. Potato Head huffed. "Who do you think you're talking to? I have over thirty accessories and I deserve more respec—" Lotso plucked off her mouth, silencing her.

"Hey! No one takes my wife's mouth! Except me!" Mr. Potato Head exclaimed as he tried to grab the mouth back. "Give it back, you furry air freshener!"

"Come on, guys," Jessie said angrily, "we're going home." She started for the door.

"Whoa there, missy!" Lotso called after her. "You're not going anywhere."

"Oh, yeah?" Jessie snapped. "And who's gonna stop us?" She turned to leave and ran smack into Buzz.

"Buzz!" Rex cheered. "You're back!" He ran to give Buzz a hug.

But when Buzz saw Rex running toward him, he struck a ninja pose. He leaped up, spinning and kicking. He knocked all of Andy's toys' legs out from under them. "Prisoners disabled, Commander Lotso!" Buzz said, snapping a salute.

"Buzz, what are you doing?" Jessie demanded.

Buzz wheeled on her. "Silence, minions of Zurg! You're in the custody of the Galactic Alliance!"

Andy's toys exchanged worried looks. *Zurg? Galactic Alliance?* Something was wrong with Buzz. He thought he was really a space ranger!

"Good work, Lightyear." Lotso patted Buzz on the back. "Now lock 'em up!"

"Yes, sir!" Buzz helped Lotso's gang herd the toys to a set of wire-mesh cubbies. They shoved them inside.

"Buzz?" Jessie reached a hand through the wire mesh. She put it on his shoulder. "We're your friends!"

"Spare me your lies, temptress!" Buzz said, shoving her hand away.

"Keep your paws off my wife!" Mr. Potato Head shouted as Big Baby stuffed Mrs. Potato Head into a cubby.

Big Baby grabbed Mr. Potato Head. "Hey, what are you doing? Let go of me, you drooling doofus!" cried the spud.

"I think this potato needs to learn himself some manners! Take him to the Box," Lotso told Big Baby.

As Big Baby carried Mr. Potato Head out to the playground, Barbie stepped into the classroom. "Ken? What's going on?" she asked. "What're you doing to my friends?" She looked over at the cubbies. Twitch and Chunk were laughing as they shoved the Aliens inside. Barbie was shocked.

"We're through!" she snapped at Ken. She stormed off toward the cubbies. Twitch locked her up with the others.

"Lightyear!" Lotso commanded. "Explain our overnight accommodations."

"Sir! Yes, sir!" Buzz saluted. "Prisoners sleep in their cells! Any prisoner caught outside their cell spends the night in the Box! Roll call at dusk and dawn! Any prisoner misses roll call spends the night in the Box! Prisoners don't speak unless spoken to! Any prisoner talks back spends the night—"

". . . in the Box," Jessie growled. "We get it."

Buzz whipped around to face her.

Lotso put a hand on his shoulder. "At ease, soldier!" He climbed to the top of a pile of blocks. "Listen up, folks. We got a way of doing things here at Sunnyside! If you start at the bottom and pay your dues, life here can be a dream come true! But if you break our rules, step out of line, try to check out early, well . . ." He tossed something toward them. It skidded across the floor and came to a stop right outside Jessie's cubby.

Andy's toys gasped. It was Woody's hat!

Jessie glared at Lotso. "What did you do to him?"

"Y'all get a good night's rest!" Lotso said, smiling, as he settled into the back of his truck. "You got a full day of playtime tomorrow!"

He and his gang started to laugh as they drove away. Andy's toys could hear Lotso laughing all the way back to the Butterfly Room.

CHAPTER SIX

"1-2-2-5," Woody typed on the keyboard. Bonnie's toys had led him to the computer in the kitchen. Now all Woody had to do was figure out where he was—and where Andy was. "Sy-ca-more. Okay, enter!"

Trixie the triceratops hit the Return key. A map appeared on the screen. Woody couldn't believe his eyes—Andy's house was right around the corner!

Woody did a little victory dance, then hurried over to the pet door. "Oh, hey, listen," he said to the other toys, "if any of you guys ever get to Sunnyside Daycare, you tell 'em Woody made it home!"

Bonnie's toys gasped. "You came from Sunnyside?" asked Dolly the rag doll.

The toys watch for Andy from the toy box.

Andy tries to decide what to do with his old toys.

Molly puts her Barbie into the daycare donation box.

Woody sees the garbage truck coming for his friends.

The toys arrive at Sunnyside Daycare.

Lotso is the leader of the Sunnyside toys.

Rex can't wait to play with the kids!

After playtime, the Potato Heads put themselves back together.

A little girl named Bonnie takes Woody home.

Buzz and Jessie get ready to charge.

Lotso wants Buzz to be a member of his gang.

A changed Buzz guards Jessie.

Woody tells the toys his plan.

Safe at home in Andy's room, the toys get ready for the attic.

"But how did you escape?" Trixie asked, wide-eyed.

"Well, it wasn't easy—" Woody broke off. He was getting a bad feeling. "What do you mean, 'escape'?"

"Sunnyside is a place of ruin and despair ruled by an evil bear who smells of strawberries!" Mr. Pricklepants told him in a hushed voice.

"Lotso?" Woody asked in disbelief.

"The guy may seem plush and huggable," Buttercup said. "But inside, he's a monster!"

Mr. Pricklepants pointed to the windowsill, where a broken toy clown sat, staring out the window. "Chuckles will tell you!"

"Yeah, I knew Lotso," Chuckles said. His voice was slow and sad. "He was a good toy. A friend. We had the same kid—Daisy. She loved us all, but Lotso was special. They did everything together. You've never seen a kid and a toy more in love."

Woody nodded. He knew what that was like.

"One day," Chuckles went on, "we took a drive. At a rest stop, we had a little playtime. After lunch, Daisy fell asleep. She never came back. . . ."

The clown explained that Daisy's parents had driven away without her toys. He and Lotso and Big Baby had waited and waited, but they didn't return.

So the three toys set off to find her house. "Lotso wouldn't give up," Chuckles explained. "It took forever, but we finally made it back to Daisy's."

It was nighttime when they got there. Big Baby gave Lotso and Chuckles a boost up to Daisy's window. But they were too late: Daisy was tucked into bed beside a brand-new pink bear.

"Something changed that day inside Lotso," Chuckles told Woody. "Something snapped."

Big Baby wore a heart-shaped pendant with Daisy's name on it. Lotso was so furious, he ripped the pendant right off Big Baby's neck. Lotso wouldn't let Big Baby or

Chuckles go inside to Daisy. "She don't love you no more!" Lotso barked at them. "Now come on!"

"We were lost. Unloved. Unwanted," Chuckles said. "Then we found Sunnyside. But Lotso wasn't my friend anymore. He wasn't anyone's friend. He took over Sunnyside, rigged the whole system."

Chuckles reached into his front pocket. He pulled out the plastic pendant that had belonged to Big Baby. It was worn and faded, but Woody could still make out the words MY HEART BELONGS TO DAISY.

"It ain't right, what Lotso done," said Chuckles. "New toys—they don't stand a chance!"

"But my friends are in there!" Woody gasped.

"You can't go back!" Buttercup insisted.

"Returning now would be suicide," Mr. Pricklepants told Woody.

"And what about Andy?" Dolly asked.

Trixie nodded. "Isn't he leaving for college?"

Woody looked around at the toys' solemn faces. He didn't know what to do. His friends needed him. If what Chuckles said was true, Woody knew his friends would never get out of Sunnyside without his help. But Andy needed him, too. And if he didn't get home soon, Andy would be gone . . . forever.

CHAPTER SEVEN

The Caterpillar Room was dark and still. Andy's toys were locked in their cubbies. Buzz the space ranger patrolled the prison.

Bullseye looked at Woody's hat and whimpered. Jessie reached her hand through the bars to stroke his muzzle. "I miss Woody, too. But he ain't ever coming back."

The bathroom door burst open. The toy dump truck tore into the room. Lotso and the gang were in the back, whooping and hollering. The truck screeched to a stop in front of the cubbies.

"Rise and shine, campers!" Lotso sang.

Buzz snapped to attention. "Commander Lotso, sir! All quiet! Nothing to report!"

"Excellent, Lightyear!" Lotso nodded at him. "Come on, we need you back at Star Command!"

Buzz hopped into the back of the truck.

"Wait!" Mrs. Potato Head cried. "What have you done with my husband?"

Big Baby stepped forward. He tossed Mr. Potato Head onto the floor. Mr. Potato Head was covered in sand and shivering. He'd spent the night locked in the Box—the Sunnyside sandbox!

"Y'all get ready," Lotso called cheerfully. "You got a playdate with destiny."

Later that morning, Bonnie raced happily into Sunnyside. She hung her backpack on a wall of coat hooks, then rushed off to join her friends.

Woody carefully unzipped the backpack. That morning, he had sneaked inside and stowed away to get back to

Sunnyside. Now Woody peered out of the bag. When nobody was looking, he scrambled to the top of a bookshelf. He pushed aside a tile in the ceiling and climbed inside. He crawled across the ceiling, following the noise of toddlers at play.

Woody pulled a tile aside and dropped into a reading loft in a corner of the Caterpillar room. He crept to the edge and peeked down to scan the room below.

A toddler smashed the Potato Heads against the floor. Another swung Jessie around by the hair, letting her crash against a wall. Woody was horrified. It was even worse than he'd imagined!

Ding! Ding! Woody looked down. It was the toy phone that had rolled over his foot on that first day at Sunnyside. The phone rang again. Then it knocked its receiver off the cradle and rolled back into the shadows.

Confused, Woody picked up the receiver and put it to his ear. "Uh . . . hello?"

"You shouldn't have come back, cowboy," the phone said. His voice was harsh and gravelly. "They cracked down since you left. You and your friends aren't ever gettin' out of here now."

"I made it out once," Woody replied.

"You got lucky once," the phone retorted. "There's only one way toys leave this place. . . ." He rolled over to the window and gestured to Woody to see for himself. Woody peered out. In the yard, a janitor was stuffing garbage bags into a trash chute. There was a broken toy train in the trash. It was getting tossed out with the rest of the garbage.

"Poor fella," the phone said. "Trash truck comes at dawn. Then it's off to the dump."

Woody shuddered. "Look, I appreciate your concern, old-timer. But we have a kid waiting for us. Now, we're leaving, one way or another. If you'd help us, I'd sure be grateful."

The phone sighed. "Well, if you're gonna get out, first

thing you gotta get through is the doors." Woody thought about the many doors—to the playground, the classroom, the front entrance. "Locked every night, inside and out," the phone said. "Keys are left on a hook in the office."

Woody nodded. "Got it. What else?"

"Lotso has trucks patrolling all night long," the phone explained. "Hallway. Lobby. Playground."

Woody wasn't worried about that. "What about the wall?" he asked.

"Eight feet high. Cinder block. No way through it."

Woody frowned. "That's it? Doesn't seem so bad."

"It's not," the phone agreed. "Your real problem is the Monkey."

The Monkey. Woody remembered a monkey—it had been at the front desk when Andy's mom first walked into the daycare center. It had cymbals, wide eyes, and a creepy grinning face.

The phone explained how the Monkey watched the

73

security monitors all night long. "He sees everything. Classrooms. Hallways. Even the playground." Whenever the Monkey saw a toy trying to escape, he would screech and bang his cymbals loudly enough for all of Sunnyside to hear. The patrol trucks would race to stop the toy. "You can unlock doors, sneak past guards, climb the wall, but if you don't take out that monkey, you ain't goin' nowhere."

Woody thanked the phone for his help just as a teacher called for recess. Woody watched as the toddlers dropped the toys and rushed outside.

"Pssst!" Woody whispered when they were gone. "Pssst! Hey, guys!"

"Woody?" Jessie cried. She rushed over to him. The others were right behind her.

"You're alive!" Slinky cheered.

"Course I'm alive— Hey, my hat!" Woody said, taking his hat from trusty Bullseye's mouth. He looked around. "Wait—where's Buzz?"

"Lotso did something to him!" Rex exclaimed.

"He thinks he's the real Buzz Lightyear!" Slinky added.

"Oh, no," Woody groaned.

"Woody, we were wrong to leave Andy," Jessie told him. She looked down at the ground. "I was wrong."

Woody shook his head. "It's my fault for leaving you guys. From now on, we stick together."

The toys all grinned, glad to have Woody back.

"But Andy's leaving for college!" Slinky said suddenly.

Jessie gasped. "We gotta get you home before Andy leaves tomorrow!"

"Tomorrow?" Hamm repeated. "But that means—"

Woody nodded. "It means we're busting out of here tonight."

CHAPTER EIGHT

Later that night, Andy's toys watched wearily from behind bars in their cubby prison as Ken started his roll call. Big Baby and Buzz stood guard nearby.

"Cowgirl," Ken called as he walked down the line of cubbies.

"Here," Jessie growled.

"Horse."

Bullseye whinnied.

Ken kept calling out names, unaware that Woody was watching through a crack in the ceiling tiles.

"Potato Head," Ken called. "Potato Head?"

Buzz backed up and peered into Mr. Potato Head's cubby. He saw a potato-shaped lump lying under a blanket.

"Hey! Tuberous root man!" Buzz shouted. "Wake up!" When Buzz rattled the bars, a *real* potato rolled out from beneath the blanket.

"Impossible!" Buzz cried. He looked around the room and spotted Mr. Potato Head. He was at the window, struggling with the lock. "Hey!"

Buzz and Ken raced after him. Big Baby followed.

Woody smiled—the first part of the plan had worked! Once Buzz, Ken, and Big Baby were distracted, Woody leaned out from his hiding place in the ceiling. He used a bent pipe cleaner to snag the clothesline where the kids' paintings were hung.

Meanwhile, Mr. Potato Head raced to the bathroom door, but it was locked tight. Buzz, Ken, and Big Baby surrounded him.

"You're turning out to be quite the troublemaker, aren't you?" Ken snarled.

Slinky slipped out of his cubby, unseen. He reached the

middle of the room just as Woody bounced down on the clothesline. The cowboy grabbed his friend and bounced back up. Woody and Slinky crept into the space above the ceiling tiles.

As the final insult, Mr. Potato Head kicked Ken in the shin. Ken yelped and hopped up and down. "Totally! Not! Cool!" He looked up at Big Baby. "Take him back to the Box!"

Big Baby grabbed Mr. Potato Head and lifted him off the ground. "No!" Mr. Potato Head shouted. "No! Not the Box! I'm sorry! I didn't mean it!"

Woody and Slinky watched as Big Baby carried Mr. Potato Head away. Woody was impressed. That part of the plan had gone off without a hitch. He'd never realized that Mr. Potato Head was such a good actor.

Below them in the Caterpillar Room, Ken clapped Buzz on the back. "Good work, Lightyear! Resume your, uh, space guy thingy."

Buzz saluted. "Yes, sir, well-groomed man!"

Ken turned to go, but Barbie called him back. "Ken?"

Ken walked over to her cubby. "What do you want?"

"I can't take it here, Ken!" Barbie sniffled, starting to cry. "I want to go to the Butterfly Room! With you!"

Ken frowned. "Yeah, well, you should've thought of that yesterday."

"I was wrong!" Barbie looked at him with huge, tear-filled blue eyes. "I want to be with you, Ken!" She broke down, sobbing.

"Darn it, Barbie!" Ken said. "Okay, but things are complicated around here. You've got to do what I say!"

"I will, Ken!" Barbie smiled at him gratefully. "I promise!"

Ken yanked open the cubby. The rest of Andy's toys watched as Barbie climbed out, leaving them behind.

Nobody tried to stop her. It was part of the plan.

Ken took Barbie back to his dollhouse in the Butterfly

79

Room. They rode the elevator up to the living room, where racks and racks of clothes lined the walls.

"Oh, wow!" Barbie started flipping through the racks. "Look at all your clothes! Tennis whites! Mission to Mars!" She marveled at the white tennis clothes and the space costume, then pulled out a groovy suit. "Vintage Disco!"

Ken sighed. "No one appreciates clothes here, Barbie." He shook his head sadly. "No one."

Barbie put a gentle hand on his shoulder. "Ken, would you model a few outfits for me?"

Ken gaped at her. Obviously, no one had ever asked him that before.

He grabbed a few outfits and ducked into a changing room. He modeled the sixties suit with the skinny tie, the lederhosen, the scuba gear, the fringed vest. He even put on a radical eighties outfit and showed her some of his best dance moves.

Barbie laughed and applauded.

Ken grinned at her. Barbie watched as he hurried to the racks for more clothes. She smiled, knowing that this could keep him busy for a long time.

Outside on the playground, Mr. Potato Head begged Big Baby not to lock him in the Box. But Big Baby didn't care. He simply tossed Mr. Potato Head in and shut the lid.

Mr. Potato Head waited until he heard Big Baby walk away. Then he found a knot in the wooden side of the sandbox. He managed to pop it out. He put his eye in his hand and poked it through the hole. The eye looked around. All clear.

One by one, Mr. Potato Head tossed his parts through the hole. Woody's plan was going perfectly.

Leaving the Caterpillar Room, Woody and Slinky Dog crawled through the ceiling until they were over the front desk. Woody pulled back the ceiling tile. He and Slinky were right above the Monkey. He was staring at the video screen with wide eyes.

Holding Woody's ankles, Slinky lowered him headfirst toward the Monkey. Closer . . . closer . . .

Screech! Suddenly, the Monkey spun around and let out a deafening scream!

Slinky was so surprised that he slipped. He and Woody crashed onto the Monkey. They knocked the microphone for the building's intercom to the floor. With a hiss, the Monkey leaped off the desk, heading for the microphone. Woody lunged after him.

Woody grabbed the Monkey, but the Monkey bashed Woody's head between his cymbals. *Crash!*

"Go!" Woody shouted between crashes. "Get!" *Crash!* "The!" *Crash!* "Tape!"

Slinky dashed across the desk. He grabbed the end of a roll of tape with his teeth and rushed back to Woody. Together they managed to wind the tape around the Monkey. They used practically the whole roll—they even taped over the Monkey's mouth.

Slinky opened a desk drawer, and Woody dropped the Monkey inside.

"Go get the key!" Slinky said.

Woody dashed to the bulletin board. He found the key buried underneath some papers. "Bingo!"

Slinky climbed back onto the desk. He moved the security camera's joystick from side to side.

In the Caterpillar Room, Jessie and Bullseye were watching the wall-mounted camera. It moved back and forth—that was Slinky's signal. "Yodel-lay-hee-hoo!" Jessie whispered.

Hamm looked at Rex. That was their cue.

"Hey!" Hamm shouted, playing his part. "What do you think you're doing? Keep your hands off of my stuff!"

Rex put up his fists. "Make a move, Porky!"

Hamm jumped on Rex. The two toys grappled.

"Hey, hey, hey!" Buzz shouted. "No fighting! Break it up!" He opened the cubby. Hamm and Rex tumbled out.

"Take that, Walnut Brain!" Hamm shouted at Rex as he bopped him on the head. "No wonder you're extinct!"

While Buzz was distracted, trying to break up the fake fight, Jessie and Bullseye climbed up to the shelf overhead.

"Hey, you can't hit each other!" Buzz pulled the two toys apart. "That's my job!"

"Yoo-hoo!" Jessie called. When Buzz looked up, Jessie and Bullseye leaped from the shelf and slammed a clear plastic storage bin over him. Hamm and Rex hopped on top of the bin, pinning it to the floor.

"Help!" Buzz shouted, but his voice was muffled by the plastic. "Prison riot!"

Buzz charged at the side of the bin, but Hamm and Rex held it down. The bin stayed put.

Bullseye went over to a locker and pulled out a lunch box. Jessie opened it and grabbed a tortilla from inside. She slid it under the door that led to the playground. Then she knocked on the door and ran off.

Mr. Potato Head's ear heard the knock. His hand hopped over to the tortilla and dragged it back into the darkness. Then the arm stuck itself into the tortilla. The other arm did the same. Eyes, nose, ears, feet, and even the mustache all attached themselves to the flat bread.

Mr. Tortilla Head stood up. He was a little wobbly— the bread was not as solid as a potato, but it would do. He strode off toward the playground.

Meanwhile, back in the dollhouse, Ken was showing off his karate outfit. *"Hai-ya! Wah! Wha-a-a!"* he cried as he demonstrated his martial arts moves. He stopped. "Uh, Barbie?"

She had disappeared. Ken looked around.

Suddenly, Barbie jumped out from behind a clothes rack and tackled Ken, pinning him to the floor. "I don't have time for games, Ken," she snarled. "What did Lotso do to Buzz, and how do we get him back to normal?"

"You can't make me talk!" Ken cried.

It didn't take long for Barbie to rope him to a paddle with the paddle-ball string. Barbie knew that the only way to get information from Ken was to go after the thing he loved best—his clothes.

"Let's see," Barbie said as she sorted through the tidy racks. "Hawaiian surf trunks." Barbie pulled them out and heartlessly ripped them apart.

"Oh!" Ken cried out as if she'd torn his heart in two. "Barbie, those were vintage!" He took a deep breath. "It's okay! All right, go ahead, rip them—I don't care. They're a dime a dozen!"

Barbie pulled out a sequined suit. "Ooh! Glitter tux!" *Rip!* She tore it in half.

Ken groaned as she tossed the pieces at him. "Who cares? Who cares? Sequins are tacky! Who cares?"

Barbie picked up a green jacket with a high collar.

"Barbie!" Ken begged. "No, please—not the Nehru!"

"This is from, what—1967?" Barbie smiled slightly.

"The Groovy Formal Collection, yes!" Ken gasped. He could hardly breathe.

"What a shame," Barbie said, picking at the jacket's seams.

A stitch popped. Then another. It was too much for Ken. "There's an instruction manual!" he cried. "Lotso switched Buzz to Demo Mode!"

Barbie held Ken in her steely gaze. "Where's that manual?"

Back in the office, Woody poked his head out the door. A security truck patrolled the hall. Woody waited for it to pass. Then he signaled Slinky Dog, who loaded a slingshot. Slinky fired the key across the hall and under the door of the Caterpillar Room.

Jessie was waiting. She stopped the key with her boot, then picked it up.

Outside, Mr. Tortilla Head struggled to climb onto a tricycle. From the handlebars, he pulled himself onto a window ledge. He looked down into the Butterfly Room. Lotso was asleep.

Mr. Tortilla Head reached for the trike's mirror. He caught a moonbeam and flashed the light toward the Caterpillar Room.

Jessie saw the signal. She gave Mrs. Potato Head the sign, and Mrs. Potato Head unlocked the door.

Jessie, Bullseye, Mrs. Potato Head, and the Aliens slipped outside. They sneaked quietly onto the playground. They had another mission to complete.

Mr. Tortilla Head was still on the ledge when he came face to face with a pigeon. The pigeon began pecking at his tortilla.

Mr. Tortilla Head swatted at the bird. It grabbed him and dragged him along the ledge. Finally, Mr. Tortilla Head landed a good, solid kick. The bird pecked him again, then flew off.

"Yeah, fly away, ya coward!" Mr. Tortilla Head shook

his fist. Suddenly, he fell to the ground as the tortilla split into pieces. There wasn't enough tortilla left to keep him together! "Well, that's great!"

But there was enough tortilla to hold an eye and an arm together. That part got up and looked around. In a corner of the playground was a small vegetable garden.

The eye grew wide. Vegetables! Now, that was more like it.

Out on the playground, Jessie and the Aliens managed to get Mr. Potato Head's body out of the sandbox. Meanwhile, Barbie had dressed up in Ken's space suit and fooled the Bookworm into handing over the Buzz Lightyear manual. As soon as she had it, she hurried to meet up with Woody.

Back in the Caterpillar Room, Rex and Hamm were guarding Buzz when Woody, Slinky, and Barbie dropped out of the ceiling.

"Woody!" cried Rex.

When Rex and Hamm stepped to the edge of the bin to

greet Woody, Buzz saw his chance. He charged against the bin, knocking Rex and Hamm off balance. They fell over the edge, giving Buzz the chance to escape.

"Stop him!" Woody cried. "Don't let him get out!"

Buzz raced toward the door, but Hamm and Rex tackled him. Barbie rushed over with the manual.

"Quick," Woody said, "open his back! There's a switch!"

"Unhand me, Zurg scum!" Buzz shouted as they opened his compartment. "The galactic courts will show you no mercy!"

Woody flipped the switch on Buzz's back, but nothing happened. "It's not working! Why's it not working? Where's the manual?" he cried.

Hamm flipped through the booklet. "Here we go! There should be a little hole under the switch!"

"Little hole." Woody nodded. "Got it!"

"'To reset your Buzz Lightyear,'" Hamm read from the manual, "'insert paper clip.'"

There wasn't a paper clip in sight. "Rex," Woody cried, "your finger!"

"Oh!" Rex looked down. His finger was definitely small enough! He stuck it into the Reset hole.

Woody looked up at Hamm. "Okay, now what?"

"All right, let's see." Hamm turned back to the manual. "'Caution: Do not hold button for more than five seconds.'"

Beep! Buzz fell facedown onto the floor.

Everyone stared at Rex. "It's not my fault!" the dinosaur cried.

Suddenly, Buzz leaped to his feet, knocking the toys off him. He strode forward, flipped open his wrist radio, and began speaking—in Spanish! He flashed his laser on Woody. *"¿Amigo o enemigo?"* he asked.

"Uh . . . amigos!" Woody said. That was one word he knew. It was Spanish for "friend." "We're all amigos!"

Buzz walked over and kissed Woody on both cheeks. Then he wandered off, continuing to mutter in Spanish.

A toy truck rumbled on the other side of the door.

"We don't have time for this!" Woody hissed. "Come on, El Buzzo!" He grabbed Buzz by the hand and dragged him toward the playground door. They had to keep going. They would have to fix Buzz later!

CHAPTER NINE

Jessie, Bullseye, the Aliens, and Mrs. Potato Head were waiting on the playground when Woody and the rest of the gang finally caught up.

"What took you so long?" Jessie asked.

"Things got complicated," Woody told her. "Where's Potato Head?"

"We haven't seen him!" Jessie was saying, when suddenly, Buzz fell to his knees in front of her, completely lovestruck. He started whispering romantically to her in Spanish.

Jessie stared at him. "Did you fix Buzz?" she murmured to her friends.

"Eh," Hamm said with a shrug, "sort of."

"Behind you!" Mrs. Potato Head whispered. "Someone's coming!"

The toys turned. A tall figure loomed before them in the darkness. The toys saw that it had large eyes, wiry arms . . . and a familiar-looking mustache.

It was Mr. Potato Head. Except his parts weren't attached to a potato—he was using a cucumber! "You would not believe what I've been through tonight!" he griped.

Mrs. Potato Head rushed over to her husband. "Darling! Are you okay?"

"I feel fresh! Healthy!" Mr. Cucumber Head groaned. "It's terrible!"

"You've lost weight!" Mrs. Potato Head said, wrapping an arm around his tall, thin cucumber body.

Bullseye nudged Mr. Potato Head's plastic body toward him. "Ah, you're a sight for detachable eyes!" Mr. Potato Head said, putting himself back together again.

The toys began to make their way across the playground.

Dodging Lotso's patrol trucks, they ducked from one piece of playground equipment to the next.

When they came to the swing set, they heard an eerie creak.

Big Baby was sitting on the last swing. He rocked slowly back and forth, looking up at the moon.

One by one, the toys crept behind Big Baby. They tried not to make a sound.

The toys had almost made it past Big Baby when one of the Aliens tripped. He landed with a *squeak!*

Big Baby's head spun around on his neck. Woody, Bullseye, and the Aliens cowered in the shadows. The giant baby doll got up and began to walk toward the sound.

At the last second, Woody and his friends dived beneath a plastic sand bucket that had been left on the ground. Big Baby reached the spot where they'd been standing. But there was no one there. He walked away.

Quickly Woody and the others raced to meet up with the rest of the toys.

"C'mon! We're almost there!" Woody said.

They made a break for the trash chute. When they got there, Woody jumped for the handle, but he wasn't tall enough.

Buzz stepped forward, brushing Woody aside. He pressed the button to activate his voice box. *"¡Buzz Lightyear al rescate!"* There was no mistaking what Buzz meant: "Buzz Lightyear to the rescue!"

Buzz stepped to the chute. In a series of flips, he jumped up toward the lid. He grabbed the handle and yanked it down.

"Way to go, Buzz!" Woody cheered. The toys boosted one another onto the lid of the trash chute. Below them, the chute disappeared into the darkness.

"Is it safe?" Jessie asked, peering down.

"I guess I'll find out," Woody said. He let go of the rim

and started down. He slid faster and faster. At the bottom he stopped, teetering on the edge of a Dumpster. If he'd slid another inch, he would have fallen right in!

"Woody!" called Jessie. "You okay?"

"Yeah. Come on down," Woody called up. "But not all at once!"

"What'd he say?" Mr. Potato Head asked.

"I think he said, 'All at once,'" Hamm said.

"No!" Woody shouted.

But it was too late. The toys were already sliding down the chute. "Whoa! Watch out!" they cried as they tumbled together. At the bottom, they slammed into Woody, almost knocking him into the trash! At the last second, Jessie grabbed him and yanked him back from the edge.

The Dumpster in front of them had a two-sided lid. The side closer to Woody and his friends was open. All they had to do was get across and they would be free.

Woody thought hard. What they needed was a bridge.

"Slink? Think you can make it?" he asked the dog.

"I might be old, but I still got a spring in my step!" Slinky backed up. He took a running leap off the edge of the trash chute. He sailed over the open part of the Dumpster and landed on the closed lid.

"He did it!" Rex squealed. Slinky's back paws were still standing on the edge of the trash chute. His long, springy body now formed a bridge across the Dumpster.

Slinky looked back at his friends. "Okay, climb across!"

But before the toys could move, two furry pink legs suddenly stepped out of the darkness in front of Slinky. It was Lotso! And his gang was with him.

"You lost, li'l doggy?" Lotso sneered at Slinky. He gave Slinky a kick. The dog slipped, but his friends pulled him to safety.

Woody and the toys turned back to the trash chute. But just then Stretch the octopus came slithering down, blocking their exit. They couldn't escape!

"What are you all doin'?" Lotso demanded. "Runnin' back to your kid? He don't want you no more!"

"That's a lie!" Woody shouted.

"Is it?" asked Lotso. "Tell me this—if your kid loves you so much, why is he leaving? It's the same for every toy! Used and abandoned," Lotso went on. "You think you're special? You were *made* to be thrown away!"

As if on cue, a garbage truck appeared in the alley. It rumbled toward them. Andy's toys gasped.

"Now, we need toys in our Caterpillar Room," Lotso said. "And you need to avoid that truck. Why don't you come on back, join our family again?" He smiled, sure that he had Andy's toys right where he wanted them.

Jessie stepped forward. "This isn't a family, it's a prison!" she shouted. "You're a liar and a bully, and I'd rather rot in this Dumpster than join any family of yours!"

Barbie stood up next to her and declared fiercely, "Jessie's right! Authority should derive from the consent of

99

the governed! Not from the threat of force!"

Lotso shrugged. "Well, if that's what you want." He banged his cane, and Stretch began to push the toys toward the Dumpster.

Just then, Ken called out, "Barbie! Wait! Don't do this, Lotso!"

"She's a Barbie doll, Ken," Lotso sneered. "There's a hundred million just like her!"

"Not to me there's not!" cried Ken. Barbie smiled at him, her heart melting.

"Fine!" Lotso snapped. "Then why don't you join her?" Lotso shoved Ken over the edge of the Dumpster.

Andy's toys caught Ken's arms and pulled him to safety. Ken turned toward the rest of Lotso's gang. "Everyone! Listen! Sunnyside could be cool and groovy if we treated each other fairly!" He pointed at Lotso. "It's Lotso! He's made us into a pyramid and he's put himself on top! But we don't have to take it anymore!"

The gang looked at one another. Andy's toys could tell that they were weighing Ken's words. Still, no one stepped forward.

"Anyone concur with Ken?" Lotso asked as the garbage truck rumbled closer. Lotso's gang was silent.

"I didn't throw you away," Lotso snarled at Andy's toys. "Your kid did. Ain't one kid who ever loved a toy, really." He started to turn—

"Wait!" Woody yelled. "What about Daisy?"

Lotso froze. "I don't know what you're talking about," he said coldly.

"Daisy. You used to do everything with her!" Woody prompted.

"Yeah—then she threw us out!" Lotso growled. His voice was bitter.

"No, she *lost* you," Woody corrected.

"She replaced us!" Lotso cried.

"She replaced you? You turned your back on her!"

Woody declared. "You lied to Big Baby, and you've been lying ever since." Woody pulled out the pendant that Chuckles had given him. The one that read MY HEART BELONGS TO DAISY.

"Where'd you get that?" Lotso cried. His stony face was on the verge of cracking.

Lotso's gang stared at him. They had never seen Lotso get so emotional.

Woody threw the pendant toward Big Baby. It landed at his feet.

Big Baby reached down and picked up the pendant. His lip quivered. "Mama!" he cried. A tear rolled down his cheek.

Lotso knocked the pendant out of his hands. "What— you want your mommy back? She never loved you! Don't be such a baby!" He ground the pendant under the end of his cane. Then he turned to Stretch, shouting, "Push them in! Push them all in!"

But before Stretch could move, Big Baby suddenly grabbed Lotso. He raised the bear over his head. Everyone watched, stunned, as the baby doll toddled toward the edge of the Dumpster.

"Put me down, you idiot!" Lotso screeched, but Big Baby didn't listen. His face was a hard mask of anger as he tossed the pink bear into the trash.

"No!" Lotso screamed. "No! Wait!"

Clang! Baby slammed the lid closed.

The toys stared, wide-eyed. "He's gone!" gasped Rex.

Big Baby blew a raspberry at the closed Dumpster lid. Then he gurgled and cooed . . . and, for the first time since Andy's toys had met him, Big Baby smiled.

Vroom! The garbage truck pulled up to a Dumpster nearby. Theirs was next!

"Come on!" Woody cried. "Hurry!"

The toys raced across the Dumpster lid to the outside wall of the trash area.

Squeak!

At the sound, Woody turned. One of the Aliens was stuck! He was struggling to free himself from the crack between the two sides of the Dumpster's lid. Woody hurried to help him.

Woody yanked the Alien free, and the three-eyed space creature dashed after the rest of Andy's toys. Woody started to follow, but now *his* foot was caught. He looked down and saw a pink paw clutching his leg!

Woody's friends watched in horror as Lotso pulled Woody into the Dumpster.

Just then, the truck arrived. It picked up the Dumpster.

Jessie gasped. She had to save Woody! She and Buzz leaped on as the truck lifted the Dumpster into the air. The other toys followed to help. Barbie tried to go, too, but Ken pulled her back. The truck turned the Dumpster upside down. The lids swung open, and the garbage spilled into the back of the truck. The toys couldn't hold on. They all fell in!

They landed inside the dark truck, surrounded by garbage. The toys coughed and groaned.

"Is everyone okay?" Woody called out.

"Of course not, you imbecile!" Mr. Potato Head snapped. "We're doomed!"

Buzz sat up. Because he glowed in the dark, he was easy to see. All of Andy's toys clustered around him. Just then, the truck lurched to a stop. The toys could hear another Dumpster being lifted up outside. It was about to drop in more trash!

"Against the wall, everybody! Quick!" Woody yelled.

The toys pressed themselves against the wall of the truck so they wouldn't be crushed by the incoming garbage.

But Jessie's foot was stuck. She couldn't move.

"Jessie!" Buzz called. *"¿Donde estás?"*

"Buzz!" Jessie yelled.

Following the sound of her voice, Buzz leaped over to her and pushed aside the trash that was pinning her down.

He picked Jessie up and carried her out of harm's way as garbage rained down from above.

"Look out!" Mrs. Potato Head shouted suddenly. A giant TV set fell toward them. Buzz lunged forward and tossed Jessie out of the way. But he couldn't save himself. The TV crashed down on top of him.

"Buzz!" Jessie screamed.

The flow of garbage had finally stopped. Jessie and the other toys rushed forward. They began to dig through the rubble.

"I found him!" Slinky said at last.

They dragged Buzz from the pile. Buzz's eyes were closed. He was perfectly still.

"Buzz, are you okay? Buzz!" Jessie shook him.

Buzz didn't move. The toys looked fearfully at one another. Had they lost him?

Beep! Suddenly, Buzz sat up. He opened his eyes and sniffed. He noticed everyone staring at him. "That wasn't me, was it?" he asked sheepishly. He wasn't speaking Spanish anymore.

"Oh, Buzz! You're back!" Jessie cried, throwing her arms around him.

Everyone shouted, clapping Buzz on the back and cheering. They were so happy that their friend was himself again.

"So where are we now?" Buzz asked.

"In a garbage truck on the way to the dump!" Rex cried.

Buzz's face fell. That wasn't exactly the news he'd been expecting.

CHAPTER TEN

Beep, *beep, beep*. The garbage truck was backing up. It lurched to a halt, and the trash bay began to tilt. The back flap opened. Andy's toys yelled as they tumbled end over end, raining down with the rest of the trash.

Woody landed with a thud and struggled to sit up. A plastic bag blew past his face. Turning, he realized that he was atop a mountain of garbage at the center of a vast landfill. His friends surrounded him. They were all winded but okay.

Just then, the Aliens spotted a large crane in the distance. "The Claw!" they cried, toddling toward it.

"Guys, no!" Woody shouted. They had to stick together! Woody tried to go after them.

Suddenly, the three Aliens were bathed in light. A huge bulldozer was heading for them! Mrs. Potato Head screamed as the Aliens disappeared under an oncoming wave of garbage.

Another bulldozer came toward the rest of the toys, blinding them with its headlights. The toys found themselves swept up in a towering hill of garbage. The bulldozer surged forward.

"Hang on!" Woody cried as the toys tumbled in the wave of trash. They were dragged under and banged around, came to the surface, then went back under again.

Finally, the toys landed on a conveyor belt. Ahead of them was a dark tunnel.

"Woody! What do we do?" Mrs. Potato Head cried.

Woody took a deep breath. "We'll be okay if we stay—"

Whoosh! Suddenly, Slinky Dog was pulled straight up into the air. He stuck to a fast-moving conveyor belt that ran overhead.

"Slinky!" Woody cried as his friend was carried away.

A hammer near Woody's feet went shooting up. It stuck to the conveyor belt next to Slinky.

"It's a magnet!" Jessie cried. "Watch out!" All around the toys, bits of metal were pulled up to the magnetic ceiling belt.

"Don't worry, Slink!" Woody ran after him. "We'll get you down!"

From high up, Slinky could see what Woody couldn't. On the conveyor belt below, Woody and his friends were moving toward a shredder! He yelled a warning to his friends.

"Quick! Grab something metal!" Buzz yelled. He grabbed hold of a lunch box. The magnet immediately pulled Buzz and the lunch box upward.

The other toys grabbed on to whatever metal they could find, and soon they were zooming along the upper conveyor belt. They were safe!

Just then, someone cried out. "Help!" The toys looked down. Below them, Lotso was pinned under a golf bag. "I'm stuck!" he yelled. "Please help!"

Woody looked at the shredder. Lotso would get sucked in at any minute. Woody quickly made a decision.

He dropped back down onto the conveyor belt and ran to help Lotso. He tried to lift the golf bag, but it was too heavy. Buzz raced to help him. Finally, the two friends managed to get the bag off Lotso. They were inches from the shredder when Woody took Lotso's paw. Buzz grabbed a golf club with one hand and Woody with the other. The magnet sucked all three toys into the air as the shredder chewed up the golf bag.

"Thank you, Sheriff!" Lotso said gratefully.

Woody nodded. "We're all in this together."

The toys let go of their metal objects. They dropped down to another conveyor belt.

"Woody! Look!" Rex cried. "I can see daylight!"

The conveyor belt they were on was headed toward an

opening. At the end, a yellow light glowed.

The toys stepped forward eagerly. But as they moved closer to the light, their faces fell.

"Uh, Rex," Woody said, "I don't think that's daylight."

It was the glow of a huge incinerator! And the toys were headed right for it!

"Run!" Woody screamed. They tried to run, but the conveyor belt moved faster. It was pulling them toward the fire.

Lotso spotted an emergency stop button overhead. There was a ladder leading up. Lotso grabbed the bottom rung. He struggled to pull himself up.

"Sheriff!" he called. "The button! Help me!"

Woody, Buzz, and Jessie ran back to him. They boosted him up. Lotso began to scramble up the ladder.

Below on the conveyor belt, Andy's toys were beginning to get tired. They couldn't outrun the belt much longer.

Lotso reached the top and turned. But he didn't push the

button. He looked down coldly at Andy's toys.

"Just push it!" Woody cried. "Push it!"

"Where's your Andy now?" Lotso smirked. Then he ran away.

"No!" Woody shouted as the toys tumbled over the edge of the conveyor belt.

They landed on a sloping hill of garbage, sliding toward the giant pool of fire. The toys tried to climb out, but it was impossible. They were sliding downward to the flames.

"Buzz!" Jessie cried. "What do we do?"

Buzz had no answer. He took her hand. Jessie understood then. There was no way out. She put her other arm around Bullseye. Slinky reached for Hamm, who took Rex's hand. The Potato Heads held each other, and Mr. Potato Head held Rex's other hand.

Woody looked over at his best friend. Buzz's face was grim. He reached for Woody. The friends were joined together, linked in a circle, as heat blasted their faces.

In moments, they would meet their end . . . together.

Suddenly, bright lights flooded Woody's face. He looked up. A giant metal claw was lowering toward them.

The claw plunged into the trash around the toys. It lifted them high into the air.

"The Claw!" cried the Aliens. They were in the crane driver's booth. They used the crane's controls to steer their friends to safety.

The claw set the toys safely on the ground. They coughed and groaned, but no one was hurt. Mr. Potato Head stared up at the sky. "You know all that bad stuff I said about Andy's attic? I take it all back."

The other toys agreed.

The Aliens scampered over from the crane. "You saved our lives!" Mrs. Potato Head told them.

"And we . . . are eternally grateful!" Mr. Potato Head added, scooping them up in a proud hug.

"Hey! Where's that furball Lotso?" Hamm asked. He

looked around, but the pink bear was nowhere in sight.

"Forget it, guys," Woody said. "He's not worth it."

The toys didn't know it, but a garbage truck driver had found Lotso in the trash and had fastened him to the front of his truck as an ornament. Being stuck to the grille of a truck, where he would get splattered with mud and bugs, was worse than being a toy in the Caterpillar Room. The hard-hearted bear had finally gotten what he deserved.

"Come on, Woody!" Jessie said suddenly. "We gotta get you home!"

"But what about you guys?" Woody said, hesitating. "I mean . . . maybe the attic's not such a great idea." He glanced at them uneasily. Before, he had been sure that the toys belonged where Andy wanted them. But now, he just wanted them to do what was right for them. They deserved to be happy.

"We're Andy's toys," Jessie reassured him.

"We'll be there for him," Buzz added. "Together."

Woody smiled. "I just hope he hasn't left yet," he said.

Mrs. Potato Head covered her eye. She concentrated hard, so that her other eye—the one still in Andy's room—could see what was happening. "Andy's still packing!" she announced. "But he's almost done!"

The toys looked at one another in despair. "He lives halfway across town," Hamm pointed out.

"We'll never get there in time!" Rex wailed.

Rock music sounded faintly on the morning air. The toys looked around. The garbageman who worked on Andy's street was playing a little air guitar before he climbed into his truck.

The toys smiled. This was their ticket home!

Andy was loading boxes into the car when the toys arrived. This was the toys' last chance! If they didn't get into a box soon, they'd never make it into the attic!

The toys quickly showered off with the garden hose. Then Slinky jumped up to the garage roof. The other toys climbed his springy body like a ladder and ran across the roof to Andy's window.

They scrambled to the sill and jumped down onto the floor, hurrying across the room. Quickly, Mrs. Potato Head found her eye under the bed and popped it back into place. Then the toys climbed into a box marked ATTIC. Buzz helped everyone get inside.

Everyone except Woody. He headed toward the box marked COLLEGE, then stopped to look back at his friends. He knew that this might be the last time he would ever see them. "Buzz . . ."

Buzz turned toward his good friend. Woody stretched out his hand, and Buzz shook it warmly. "This isn't goodbye," Woody said, although he feared that it was.

"Hey, Woody, " Slinky called from the ATTIC box. "Have fun at college!"

"Woody, take care of Andy," Rex added.

"Sure thing." Woody reached a hand toward Jessie.

"Jessie—you'll be okay in the attic?"

"Course I will," Jessie said.

Woody turned back to Buzz. There was so little time left. He was suddenly overwhelmed by how much he would miss his friends.

"You know where to find us, cowboy," Buzz told him. He climbed into the ATTIC box.

Woody hopped into the COLLEGE box. He lowered himself inside just as Andy and his mom walked into the room.

Andy's mom looked around the empty room. Suddenly, her eyes filled with tears. "Oh, Andy! I wish I could always be with you." She pulled him into a hug.

"You will be, Mom," Andy told her, hugging her back.

Woody stood up and peered through the box's handhold. Then he noticed a photo packed along with everything else. It was the picture of ten-year-old Andy, playing with all his toys. Andy had said that his mother would always be with him. Woody knew what Andy meant—he meant that she would always be in his heart. All this time, Woody had thought that the toys needed to be there for Andy, waiting in the attic. But really, they *would* always be there for him, no matter where they were. They would be in his heart, and in his memories.

"Hey," Molly said as she poked her head into the room. "Aren't you gonna say goodbye to Buster?"

"Of course I am!" Andy stepped into the hall to pet the dog. "Who's a good doggie? I'm gonna miss you!"

While Andy was gone, Woody scrambled out of the box. He picked up a pen and scribbled on a sticky note. He stuck it on the ATTIC box.

Woody slipped out of sight just as Andy came back into the room.

"Okay, Buster, now don't let Molly near my stuff," Andy said. He crouched down to pick up the ATTIC box and noticed the sticky note. "Hey!" He opened the box. He was surprised—and happy—to see all his toys.

Andy reread the note. "Hey, Mom," he called over his shoulder. "So you really think I should donate these?"

"It's up to you, honey," his mom called from the hall. "Whatever you want to do."

Woody held his breath. He didn't know what Andy would do. Maybe he'd still keep everyone in the attic.

All Woody could do was hope. . . .

CHAPTER ELEVEN

Andy stopped the car in front of a pretty little house and looked at the address on the gate. Then he checked the address on the sticky note. "1225 Sycamore."

Andy paused a moment. Then he grabbed the box on the seat next to him and started up the front walk.

Bonnie was in the front yard, playing. Her mom and dad were working in the garden nearby. "No!" Bonnie cried. "Don't go in there! The bakery is haunted! Look out! The ghosts are throwing pies! *Splat! Splat! Splat!*"

Bonnie looked up in surprise as Andy walked toward her. "Mom?" she called.

Bonnie's mom looked over. "Andy!"

"Hi!" He let himself in at the gate.

"Wow! Look at you!" Bonnie's mom beamed. "I hear you're off to college?" Bonnie hid behind her mom.

"Yeah. Right now, actually. Uh . . . I have some toys here." Andy held out the box.

"Oh! You hear that, Bonnie?" asked her mother. Bonnie peeked around her mom, suddenly interested.

Andy crouched down so that he was eye to eye with the little girl. "So you're Bonnie? I'm Andy," he said. "Someone told me you're really good with toys. These are mine, but I'm going away now, so I need someone really special to play with them."

He sat down and pulled Jessie and Bullseye out of the box. "This is Jessie, the roughest, toughest cowgirl in the whole West. She loves critters, but none more than her best pal, Bullseye. *Yee-haw!* Here." He held Jessie and Bullseye out to the little girl.

Bonnie smiled. She took the toys as Andy pulled a dinosaur out of the box.

"This is Rex—the meanest, most terrifying dinosaur who ever lived. *Rawr!*" Andy thrust Rex at Bonnie. Rex had never looked fiercer! Bonnie backed up a moment, then grinned and took the dinosaur.

"The Potato Heads—Mister and Missus," Andy said as he pulled them from the box. "You gotta keep them together 'cause they're madly in love." Bonnie nodded seriously as Andy went on. "Now, Slinky here is as loyal as any dog you could want. But Hamm? You gotta watch this guy." He'll keep your money safe, but he's also one of the most dastardly villains of all time . . . evil Dr. Porkchop!"

Next, Andy removed the Aliens. "These little dudes are from a strange, alien world—Pizza Planet! And this is Buzz Lightyear—the coolest toy ever. Look—he can fly." Andy deployed Buzz's wings. "And shoot lasers. He's sworn to protect the galaxy from the evil Emperor Zurg!" Andy handed Buzz over. Bonnie pressed the red button on Buzz's chest.

"Buzz Lightyear to the rescue!" Buzz's voice box said.

"Now, you gotta promise to take good care of these guys," Andy said. "They mean a lot to me."

Bonnie smiled at him. She glanced into the box, and her eyes went wide. "My cowboy!"

Andy looked down. Woody was lying in the box. "What's he doing in there?" he said as he picked Woody up.

"There's a snake in my boot!" Bonnie cried.

Andy blinked at her. Then he pulled Woody's string. "There's a snake in my boot!" Woody's voice box said.

Bonnie giggled, reaching for Woody. Andy hesitated. Finally, he sighed and held out the cowboy.

"Now, Woody, he's been my pal for as long as I can remember," Andy told Bonnie. His voice was gentle and serious. "He's brave, like a cowboy should be. And kind, and smart. But the thing that makes Woody special? He'll never give up on you. He'll be there for you, no matter what. You think you can take care of him for me?"

Bonnie nodded solemnly.

"Okay, then." Andy handed Woody to Bonnie. She gave Woody a huge hug.

Andy smiled at her, then grabbed Hamm. "Oh, no! Dr. Porkchop's attacking the haunted bakery!" He made laser-gun sounds. *"Pchoo! Pchoo!"*

"Oh, no!" Bonnie chimed in. "The ghosts are getting away! Woody to the rescue!"

Woody couldn't remember ever having a better playtime. Maybe it felt special because all his friends were there. Or maybe it was special because all Bonnie's toys were there, too. But Woody knew that the most special part was that it was the last time he'd ever get to play with Andy.

Finally, Andy had to say goodbye. He climbed into his car and took one last look at all his toys. They were safely on Bonnie's porch. Woody was in her arms.

"Bye, guys," Andy said softly, to himself. Then he pulled away.

Bonnie turned to her mother. "Look, Mommy! New toys!" She put Woody down and ran over to give her mother a hug.

"Come on," her mother said. "Let's get some lunch." She scooped her daughter into her arms and swung her around. Bonnie laughed as they went into the house.

The toys sat up. They watched as Andy drove away.

"So long, partner," Woody said sadly.

Buzz put his arm around Woody. The other toys gathered close as Andy rolled out of sight. They had one another. And now they had Bonnie and some new toy friends.

But they would always love Andy . . . because he had loved them first.